The Night the Tooth Fairy Did Not Come
by
Amy Lynn Louhela

Illustrated by Lily Todorova

Amy would like to dedicate this book to:
Maykia and Isa the start of my inspiration.
Myrissa, Tanner, Tristan, for all the times the tooth fairy did not arrive.
To Calyb my beautiful Grandson.
To my nieces and nephews.
To my parents Reinhold and Autumn.
To my in-laws Char and Dan.
To Kyle the love of my life.
And last but not least to the wonderful staff members at
Wyndham resort in Branson,Mo. Marissa and Jesse
who helped edit my book!!

Lily would like to dedicate this book:
To my little sister, Teddy,
who believes that I can draw anything,
for her endless love and support.
To my parents, Nadya and Anton,
who bought me countless books throughout my childhood.
And to my grandma Lily,
who used to tell me fairytales when I was young!

1

The sun rose in the sky
and Lily opened her big brown eyes.
The morning she had waited for was here.

3

Lily searched and proclaimed
" How can this be,
the tooth fairy did not take my tooth
from me? "

Lily pondered and thought
and then it came to her mind,
"The tooth fairy must have been in a bind..."

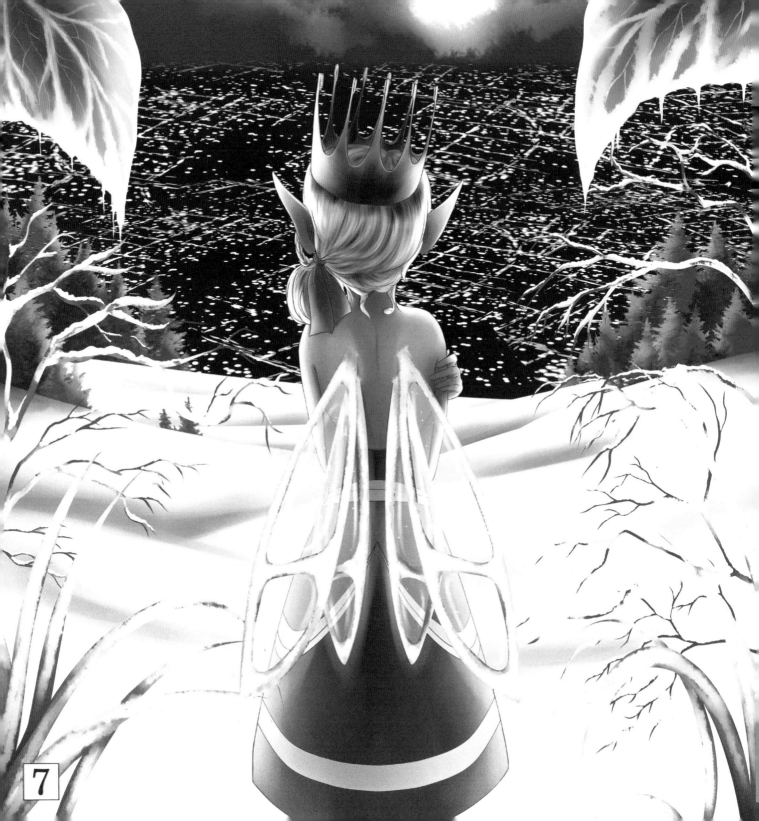

Perhaps the cold winter night had caused her wings to lose flight.

Maybe the warmth of the air
had caused her wings not to flare.

11

Maybe she was held at bay and left with no dollars or coins to pay.

Maybe the day was long,
her babies didn't sleep,
she overslept and missed her keep.

Perhaps she was ill and unable to perform the task she had to fulfill.

The growing concern caused Lily
to ask her mother to discern
"Mommy, Mommy how can this be?
Why did the tooth fairy not take
the tooth from me?"

Lily's mother
quite shocked and surprised
also assumed the fairy must have been
in a bind.
"Lily my dear do not fret
the tooth fairy is bound
to come yet."

With faith and assurance,
Lily made it through the day
knowing the tooth fairy always
has lots of courage.

The night sky was about to begin
and Lily knew that in a short time
the tooth fairy surely would sweep in.

Lily drifted off to sleep
without making a peep.

Lily woke up in the morning,
looked under her pillow and proclaimed
"Thank you tooth fairy for being so kind!
I'm happy you brought me
nickels and dimes!"

The Night The Tooth Fairy Did Not Come

First Published by Amy Louhela 2014

Copyright © Amy Louhela, 2014

Original Illustrations Copyright © Liliya Todorova, 2014

ISBN: 978 -1496057112

Amy Louhela

334 8th St.

Cloquet, MN 55720

United States of America

amylouhela@yahoo.com

Printed in the United States of America

First Printing, 2014

31483498R00020

Made in the USA
Lexington, KY
13 April 2014